Dear Molly, Dear Olive

Molly Discovers Magic
(Then Wants to Un-discover It)

written by
Megan Atwood

illustrated by
Lucy Fleming

PICTURE WINDOW BOOKS
a capstone imprint

Dear Molly, Dear Olive is published by Picture Window Books,
a Capstone Imprint
1710 Roe Crest Drive
North Mankato, Minnesota 56003
www.mycapstone.com

Copyright © 2017 Picture Window Books

Library of Congress Cataloging-in-Publication Data
Names: Atwood, Megan, author. | Fleming, Lucy, illustrator.
Title: Molly discovers magic (then wants to un-discover it) / by Megan Atwood;
[illustrated by Lucy Fleming].
Description: North Mankato, Minnesota: Picture Window Books, an imprint of Capstone Press,
[2017] | Series: Dear Molly, Dear Olive | Summary: After a string of incredibly good luck,
Molly decides that she has developed magical powers—but when she finds out that her pen
pal Olive has had an equally surprising run of minor disasters Molly starts to wonder if her
magical good luck is somehow responsible for her friend's problems.
Identifiers: LCCN 2016010937 | ISBN 9781479586943 (library binding) |
ISBN 9781623706166 (paperback) | ISBN 9781479586981 (eBook (pdf))
Subjects: LCSH: Best friends—Juvenile fiction. | Pen pals—Juvenile fiction. | Letter
writing—Juvenile fiction. | Magic—Juvenile fiction. | Coincidence—Juvenile fiction. |
Fortune—Juvenile fiction. | New York (N.Y.)—Juvenile fiction. | Iowa—Juvenile fiction. |
CYAC: Best friends—Fiction. | Friendship—Fiction. | Pen pals—Fiction. | Letter writing—
Fiction. | Magic—Fiction. | Coincidence—Fiction. | Luck—Fiction. | New York (N.Y.)—
Fiction. | Iowa—Fiction.
Classification: LCC PZ7.A8952 Mo 2017 | DDC 813.6—dc23
LC record available at http://lccn.loc.gov/2016010937

Designers: Aruna Rangarajan and Tracy McCabe

Design Elements: Shutterstock

Printed in Canada.
009642F16

Table of Contents

Dear Molly,
Dear Olive

Molly and Olive are best friends — best friends who've never met! Two years ago, in second grade, they signed up for a cross-country Pen Pal Club. Their friendship was instant.

Molly and Olive send each other letters and email. They send postcards, notes, and little gifts too. Molly lives in New York City with her mom and younger brother. Olive lives on a farm near Sergeant Bluff, Iowa, with her parents. The girls' lives are very different from one another. But Molly and Olive understand each other better than anyone.

Chapter 1

Magic Powers

Molly

Dear Olive,

How are you? I am MAGICAL.

I don't remember getting struck by lightning. Or getting bitten by anything. I didn't open any books of magic spells. But two days ago, everything I thought about came true.

On Monday, I dreamed about cupcakes. They were chocolate, with the best frosting ever. Guess what? Tuesday someone brought cupcakes to class! They looked EXACTLY like the ones I dreamed about.

Then, after school, the sun was so bright it hurt my eyes. I wished for rain. TWO HOURS LATER it rained.

I didn't do my homework last night. I knew I was going to be in trouble this morning. But before I could tell my mom, she came into my room. She said, "School's closed because of a gas leak."

Can you believe that?

So there you have it. I am now a magical person. However I got this magical power, I know I have to be careful. Being a magical person comes with a lot of responsibility, I think.

Maybe when I get the hang of this, I can wish for things for you too!

Your best friend,

Molly

~ Molly ~

I folded my letter to Olive and sealed the envelope. I got out the book of stamps. Only one stamp left. Perfect. Magic!

My little brother, Damien, ran into my room and slid across the floor. He jumped and landed with a bounce on my bed. First of all, he's not supposed to be in my room. Second, Mom doesn't allow jumping on the beds.

"Get out of my room," I said.

Normally Damien would stick out his tongue at me. But this time he actually got off my bed. I was a little amazed, but I tried not to show it. As he walked out the door, I yelled, "Don't trip on your way out!"

THAT'S when he turned around and stuck out his tongue at me. Then he giggled and started running away.

But then . . . the magic got him.

Damien turned right, but his feet turned left.
He fell on the floor with a loud *THWUNK!*

It had to be because of what I'd said! Magic!

He was trying hard not to cry, I could tell.
He is only six years old after all. At ten years
old, I'd never cry at something like that. I am
not a baby.

"I'm sorry, Damien," I said.

He sat up and rubbed his backside. Then he looked at me with his eyes all squinty. "Boogerface," he said.

He was okay.

I stepped back and shrugged. "You forgot to pack your bags," I said.

He stood up and scrunched his face. "What do you mean?" he asked.

I punched him in the shoulder. "For the trip you just took!"

"MOM!" Damien yelled.

The next day during library hour, I knew exactly what I had to do.

I marched up to Ms. Hill, the librarian. She didn't look up. I stood there for a moment, then I cleared my throat real loud. "AHEM!"

She looked up. Magic!

"Ms. Hill," I said, "I have a very important question for you."

She smiled at me and nodded.

"If I wanted to learn about magic," I continued, "what book would I look up?"

"Well," she said, "we have *How to Do Magic Tricks* over in the how-to section."

I shook my head. "No, different magic. REAL magic."

Ms. Hill looked at me, puzzled. "I'm not sure what you mean, Molly."

I leaned in and whispered, "I mean, Ms. Hill, if someone I knew had magic powers, where could she learn about how to control them?"

I could have really hurt Damien when he tripped. What if I couldn't get control of my magic and I hurt someone else?

"I see," she said. "Yes, we might have just the thing for you."

I think librarians have their own magic.

Chapter 2

Nothing But Bad Luck

Olive

I took the package from the postal worker. "Damaged?" I said.

She shrugged and smiled. "Sorry, Olive. It had to come back to you because it is too damaged to send." Then she walked back to her truck, leaving me with a wrecked package.

It was a complete mess. I really hoped the T-shirt inside — the one I'd made for Molly — wasn't ruined. I put the package under my arm and walked up the stairs to my house.

Except I didn't exactly walk. I fell. UP the stairs. I just stared at the wood boards below me. My knees hurt. My palms hurt. I didn't even want to get up. I'd had the worst day already. What was happening?

In the morning I had helped Dad milk the goats and accidentally left the pen open. One of them had eaten right through a shirt hanging on the clothesline.

And now this! A totally ruined package and me falling on my face.

I picked myself up and brushed off the

dirt. I hoped I wouldn't be this clumsy at the gymnastics meet tonight. We were up against Des Moines. They were SUPER tough.

I grabbed the package and walked into the house, limping a little. I flopped down on one of the big comfy chairs in our living room. My knee hurt a lot. Rolling up my jeans, I saw that I'd skinned it.

This was the WORST day.

I took the T-shirt out of the packaging. The shirt was all in one piece, but there was a huge black tire mark right down the center. I'd taken a Sioux City Gymnastics T-shirt and written

Molly's name on the back. Like she was on our team. I wrote it in bright puffy-paint letters. My mom had gotten the puffy paint especially for Molly's T-shirt. When I flipped the shirt over, the name was peeling off.

My note to Molly was torn in two. Now it just said:

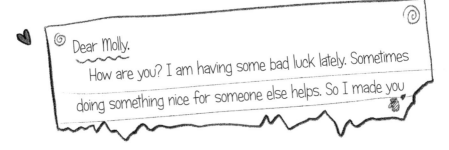

Dear Molly,
How are you? I am having some bad luck lately. Sometimes doing something nice for someone else helps. So I made you

The rest of the note was probably flying across a cornfield.

Dad came in and saw me with my jeans rolled up and the T-shirt in my hand. "Hey, Peanut," he said. "Rotten day?"

I nodded. "I'm having the WORST luck today, Dad."

"Well," he said, "I hope this bad luck doesn't stick around for the meet. Speaking of which, you need to change clothes right now. We have to get going!"

I raced to my room and put on my uniform. It was time to turn this bad luck around.

Both Dad and Mom were waiting for me. My knee still hurt a little bit, but now I was excited for the meet.

"Hey, Olive," Mom said, "you have a letter here from Molly. It looks like something ran over it."

Sure enough, the envelope had a tire mark on it. It matched my damaged package.

"When did this come?" I asked. "I just met Cheryl out on the street. That's when she gave me the damaged package."

Mom shook her head. "I don't know. It was in today's mail pile. You can read it when you get home. Right now we have to fly out of here to make it to your meet."

I put the letter down on the table by the door, and we all went out to the truck.

The meet started, and I forgot about my bad luck. When it was my turn on the beam, I took a deep breath and jumped up. I felt steady. Solid. I did a back handspring. And another back handspring. I did a couple jumps.

Then it was time for my dismount.

I had done everything perfectly so far. Now all that was left was my back tuck. Coach always said the landing was the most important part.

I stepped to the end of the beam . . .

launched . . .

and landed flat on my belly.

I scrambled to my feet and put my arms up. Tears stung my eyes. I'd belly flopped! On a simple back tuck. I do those all the time! Talk about bad luck. I'd probably ruined the chances for my team to win the meet.

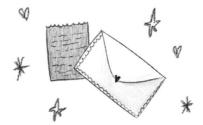

When I got off the mat, the tears came
loose. Coach put his arm around me.
My teammates patted my shoulders.

I couldn't look at any of them. All I wanted
to do was go home and go to bed.

We lost the meet.

On the drive home, I looked out the window
and didn't say anything. Mom and Dad felt
bad for me. But there was nothing
we could do now.

We pulled up to the
house, and that's when
I remembered — I'd
forgotten my homework!
Ugh! Could this day get
any worse?

That's when I noticed the car in the driveway. "Who's here?" I asked.

Mom smiled. "Oh," she said, "I forgot to tell you. Great-Aunt Gladys is visiting! She'll be staying in your room."

Yep. The day COULD get worse.

When we walked inside, Great-Aunt Gladys was sitting in the rocking chair. She saw me and said, "Stand up straight, Ms. Olive. This isn't a slouching competition."

I looked at my mom. She nodded. I had to get out of there. I ran to Great-Aunt Gladys, gave her a peck on the cheek, and grabbed Molly's letter.

"Olive just finished a meet, Gladys," Mom said. "She's a little tired. Let's let her get settled while George and I make dinner. You can sit in the kitchen so we can catch up."

I barely heard the last part. I was running away too fast.

I ripped open Molly's letter and read it. She was having the complete OPPOSITE of bad luck. She was having nothing but GOOD luck. I was super happy for her. I had to tell her about what was going on with me though. I needed my best friend to cheer me up.

No time for a paper letter. I got on my computer. It was times like these that I wished we hadn't agreed to not talk on the phone.

Hi, Molly!

I got your letter. That sounds great! What do you think you'll do with your new magic?

I'm having a string of bad luck. I bombed at my meet today. The goats got out of the pen. The package I sent you got run over and sent back to me. I forgot my homework.

And my stuffy GREAT-AUNT GLADYS is here. And she's taking over my room!

I really hope my luck changes soon. Send me luck! And have fun with your new magic. ☺

Love,

Olive

Chapter 3

Magic Mysteries Solved

Molly

Ms. Hill led me to a book called *Histories of Ancient Civilizations*. She patted me on the head and said, "I'm sure this has some 'real' magic in it." Then she walked away to answer another question.

History? Ancient civilizations? Boring.

Maybe librarians weren't magic after all.

But then I saw a book that was perfect. It was stuck between the boring one and another one. The spine was all worn, but I could see it peeking out between both books. I saw the letters M-A-G.

That was a good start.

It was WAY up high. I got a step stool, but the shelf still wasn't eye level. I reached up blindly and grabbed. Then I pulled.

The book was really stuck. So I cleared my mind, squinted my eyes, and tried to bring up my magic.

I pulled again . . . and got it! Magic!

I also fell off the step stool, but I landed on my feet. Magic again!

The book was a very thin paperback. *Magic Mysteries Solved: How to Use Magic in Your Life.* The cover had a picture of sparkles and a wand on it.

I clutched the book to my chest and walked over to my favorite beanbag chair. Janice was sitting in it. I cleared my throat loudly. She grabbed her books and got up.

Everyone knew that was my beanbag chair.

I flopped down, peeled the book away from my chest, and opened it. First I read the Table of Contents:

Holy buckets! The book had everything I wanted. I settled into the chair and started reading. I took out a notebook to take notes.

I read through the whole class period. When the bell rang, I still had three chapters to go. Ms. Hill came over, and I hid the book under my legs.

"Time to go, Molly," she said. She looked at me like she knew I was hiding something. But she left pretty quick.

When she turned her back, I tucked the book under the beanbag chair. I couldn't take the chance that someone else would find it on the shelf. And I couldn't check it out. I didn't want anyone to know about my powers yet. I'd just have to come back tomorrow and read the final chapters. In the meantime I closed my notebook and left the library.

I couldn't WAIT to get home to read through my notes.

I stared at Olive's email. She had NO magic in her life lately.

I knew why.

I grabbed my notebook and flipped through it. I read the notes that seemed to make the most sense:

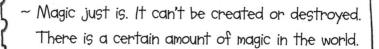

~ Magic just is. It can't be created or destroyed. There is a certain amount of magic in the world.

~ Everyone has magic. Some people have more than others.

~ Magic normally begins when you're young.

That one didn't apply to me. I was already ten years old. I kept reading.

~ Magic is hard to control, but it's possible.

~ Magic can *hurt* as well as *help* people.

I closed the notebook and chewed my lip. If the book was right, I had more magic than Olive did. What if I had stolen Olive's magic?

My eyes went wide. It was the only thing that made sense. How else could my new good luck be explained? And Olive's terrible luck?

Olive and I wrote to each other all the time. Maybe in one of our emails or letters, I had zapped all her magic.

Not cool.

I had to tell her. I slid into my desk chair and started an email.

Dear Olive,

Well, you're never going to believe this. But I think I might have stolen your magic. It was an accident! You have to believe me. Don't worry — I'm going to fix it —

I stopped and glanced at my notes. *Maybe I shouldn't say anything to her until I have a plan,* I thought. What a better email that would make! Right now, an email about her stolen magic might just get her mad.

I couldn't stand the thought of Olive being mad at me.

I clicked off the computer and sat back. Tomorrow, during reading time, I would finish that book. And I WOULD fix Olive's magic problem.

A Cat, a Dog, and Two Itchy Legs

Olive

After the sixth cheek pinch from Great-Aunt Gladys, I had to get out of the house.

"I'm going to milk the goats, Mom," I yelled from the living room. It didn't matter that I'd already milked them that morning.

"Olive, it's not ladylike to play with goats!" Great-Aunt Gladys said.

The goats could be annoying, but they were better than Great-Aunt Gladys.

I bounced out the front door, letting the screen door slam. One of our barn cats, Stella, came and rubbed up against me. We had three cats, but Stella was my favorite. When my parents weren't looking, sometimes I let her inside to sleep with me.

I reached into my pockets and gave her a couple treats. I picked her up. Stella always made me feel better.

But then my rotten luck struck again.

Our neighbor's dog, Beano, came running out of nowhere, right down our driveway.

A *good* farm dog knows not to go after small animals. You can't have a farm dog who eats your chickens.

Or cats.

Beano was *not* a good farm dog.

Stella saw Beano coming. She growled low in her throat. I tried to hold on to her so she wouldn't run — dogs love to chase things — but Stella wasn't having it.

With a loud cat scream and a whir of claws, Stella freaked out. She used me as a jumping board and sprang away.

I felt the scratches right away. But worse, Beano started chasing Stella.

So, of course, I started chasing Beano.

That dumb dog barked and barked and ran all over. I couldn't keep up!

I ran through a small forest of green stuff near our treeline and lost Beano and Stella along the way. I stopped to get my breath.

Then I heard Beano barking again. I ran farther into the trees and saw that Stella had climbed one. She was sitting on a branch, hissing and swiping at Beano.

"Beano!" I yelled. "Go home!"

Beano stopped, cocked his head, and took off toward his home. Stella's eyes were huge. Her ears lay all the way back. I reached in my pocket and grabbed a treat.

She growled a little, but I got her to jump down. That's when I felt strange prickles on my ankles. I'd been too worried about Stella to notice before.

I looked down.

I was standing in a patch of poison ivy.

Bad luck had struck again.

I lay on the couch, my lotion-covered legs sticking up to the ceiling. Great-Aunt Gladys talked on and on about how in her day, girls didn't wear short shorts. That's why I got the poison ivy rash, she said.

"Gladys," Mom said, "why don't we let Olive rest for a bit. George is going to run you into town to do some shopping. There's that store you like in the mall, remember?"

Great-Aunt Gladys smiled. "Yes," she said. "Oh, a delightful little store. So many cute, colorful things."

My dad walked in and winked at me. I think Great-Aunt Gladys might have been getting on his nerves too.

 "All right, George," Great-Aunt Gladys said. "Let's go to that shop. Maybe we can get something for our poor Olive here."

Well. Okay. Maybe Great-Aunt Gladys wasn't ALL bad.

As soon as they left, Mom sat down by me. "Bad day, huh?" she said. "Anything I can do for you, little lamb?"

I swallowed back tears. Bad DAYS — more than one. But I didn't say anything. She wouldn't believe I was cursed with rotten luck. Only Molly would understand.

Molly. Maybe Molly could help!

"Mom, can you bring me my laptop?" I asked. "I'd go get it from my room, but I'd get lotion on everything."

She patted my head. "Sure, honey." Then, because she always seems to know what I'm thinking, she said, "Molly will help. Best friends often do."

Minutes later I was clicking keys like crazy.

Hey, Molly!

How are you? I'm not doing so great. Things keep getting worse and worse. I'm covered in an itchy rash. FROM POISON IVY. Long story.

I had an idea. Could you lend me some of your magic? I wouldn't need a lot — just enough so that everything isn't horrible.

What do you think?

Love,

Olive

    Molly must have been on the computer at the same time. I got an answer in three minutes! I know it was exactly three minutes. I watched the clock on the computer. It felt like five years.

Dear Olive,

I was thinking the EXACT same thing. I'm working on it, I promise. I found a good book. I think I can fix your luck problem. Give me a little time.

I'm SO sorry about everything.

Love,

Molly

Whew! But why was Molly sorry? It wasn't HER fault I had bad luck. I wrote her a quick email to thank her and tell her what a great best friend she was.

Chapter 5

A Heart Split in Two

Molly

The book didn't help at all. It said magic was unequal sometimes — more in one place than another. But it didn't say ANYTHING about how to make it equal again.

I'd snuck the book out of school in my backpack. I wasn't stealing it. Just borrowing it. Until I didn't need it anymore. Then I'd put it back where I found it.

I picked up my notebook.

I'd written down my day to see how the magic was working.

> Magic Notes:
>
> 8:30 Made Damien drop his spoon in his cereal. Milk splashed into his face. Funny.
>
> 8:40 Sat in my room and thought extra hard about good things happening to Olive. ♥

I took out my pen and added a note to that one: DIDN'T WORK. Maybe it was because Olive lived so far away.

> 9:30 Got an A on my math test.
>
> 10:45 Got the tetherball first at recess.
>
> 12:00 Had my favorite lunch — pizza!
>
> 3:15 Grams picked me up from school and took me and Damien for ice-cream cones. "Just because."

5:00 Mom made my favorite dinner. Damien didn't throw anything at me.

7:00 Mom said I could watch TV for TWO HOURS because I'd been picked grade ambassador.

It had been a good day. But all because I'd stolen the magic from my best friend.

I felt the necklace around my neck — the one that said FRIENDS. Olive had the other half of the necklace. Her half said BEST.

My best friend was counting on me. Not only did I steal her magic, I also couldn't fix it! What kind of a best friend was I? I didn't even deserve that necklace.

Then I remembered something from the book I'd read. I flipped through the pages, stopping at the chapter about responsibility.

It said, "Not only are your thoughts magical, but objects that touch you become more magical too. Especially if they are close to your heart. The Magic-User must be extra careful about loaning these things."

I opened up my computer.

Dear Olive,

I think I've got it! I'm going to send you my necklace. You send me yours. I think this will give you some of my magic and turn your luck around!

Love,

Molly

I carefully wrapped my necklace and slid it into an envelope. I'd mail it in the morning.

Two days later, I got Olive's necklace and a note that said THANK YOU in huge letters. I wore the necklace to school and kept feeling the half of the heart with my fingers. At first, everything seemed fine.

Then everything fell apart.

At library hour, Janice was in my beanbag chair again. "AHEM," I said. She sighed and moved to get up.

But then Ms. Hill came out of nowhere. "Molly, I think you should shake it up a little, don't you?" she said. "Why don't you sit over there today?"

Ms. Hill had her "Don't argue" look on. So I didn't argue. Janice smiled at me in a "ha-ha" way. SO not fair.

Ms. Hill made me sit in a circle of beanbag chairs, so I didn't even get my own spot. I had to listen to Tyler, Trent, and Jenny talk about some dumb video game I don't play.

By the end of the school day, I was sitting outside Principal Martinez's office. I was in trouble. I was trying super hard not to cry.

I touched Olive's necklace around my neck.

Well, at least I knew where all my magic had gone.

WRITE SOON

Chapter 6

✳ Good Luck Returns

Olive

I watched as Dad put the last of Great-Aunt Gladys' things in the car.

"I wish I could stay longer," she said. "It's been a delightful visit."

I couldn't help it. I did a little happy dance, right there on the front porch.

"Stand up straight, Olive," Great-Aunt Gladys called from the car. "Remember, ladies don't slouch!"

I put on a huge smile and waved really big.
"Goodbye, Great-Aunt Gladys! Have a safe
drive home!"

When her car pulled out of the driveway,
I ran up to my room and jumped on my bed.
My bed again!

I touched Molly's necklace. It was all
because of her. Molly was magical. For real!
I needed to write to her and let her know how
great things had been ever since she sent it.

But first I had another
gymnastics meet.

"Olive, let's go!" Mom yelled.

I changed into my uniform fast and ran downstairs. As I shot out the door, at the very last minute, I noticed Stella on the front step. Luckily I saw her in time and jumped over. I landed perfectly on my feet.

Stella made a surprised *CHIIIRP!* sound at me, and I laughed. Just one day ago, I would have stepped right on her. With my bad luck? You bet! But not now, not with this necklace.

My parents and I got to Sioux City in plenty of time. Mom said it was weird that there wasn't much traffic. But I knew the reason. Magic! Inside my head I thanked Molly.

I walked into the gym and breathed deep. That's when I remembered our meet was

against Holstein. They had the best balance beam performer in the area. At least that's what all the newspapers said. Her name was Layna Chu.

I'd be going up against her.

I felt Molly's necklace in my fingers. Today was the wrong day for that poor girl. I had magic on my side.

Later my teammates and I watched Layna perform. She was good.

"It's okay if you don't beat her score, Olive," my captain said. "I think we have enough points to edge them out. So don't feel bad."

GO OLIVE!

I just smiled at her and said, "Oh, I don't think we'll have to worry about that."

When it was my turn, I felt Molly's necklace one last time. Then I took it off and gave it to my coach.

I jumped onto the balance beam. Then I did two — two! — back handsprings. I did turns and leaps. I didn't wobble a bit.

Before I knew it, it was time for my dismount. Thoughts of last meet's horrible belly flop popped into my head. But I had Molly's magic on my side this time.

I landed perfectly. Magic!

The whole place exploded with cheers. My teammates went wild. They slapped me on the back. Coach yelled, "YES, YES!" My parents shouted, "WHOOO-HOOOO!" I smiled so wide it felt like my face would split in two.

I watched as our points added up. I looked at my score compared to Layna's.

I'd scored higher. And I knew exactly why.

After a shower and some dinner, I wrote an email to Molly.

Dear Molly,

You are the best friend I could ever have. Guess what? You DID give me some of your magic. I just got done with the best gymnastics meet of my life. Great-Aunt Gladys is gone. So is the rash from the poison ivy. And at school today, I got all As. It's because of your necklace!

Thank you for helping me!

Love,

Olive

I went to bed feeling pretty good. Now Molly and I had the same magic. We were back on track. Nothing but good luck for us both!

Because of the Magic

Molly

For the second time in two days, I sat in Principal Martinez's office. She frowned at me. It was like we were having the same day over and over again.

She raised her eyebrows. "Well?" she said. "What happened this time?"

Yesterday I'd lifted up the beanbag chair that Janice had been sitting in and dumped her out of it.

Today the tetherball hit me in the head. Hard. So I ripped it down from the pole.

Two days of bad luck. Two days in the principal's office.

Part of me was mad at Olive for this bad luck. A LOT of me wanted my necklace back. But that would mean Olive would have bad luck again. I didn't want that either.

Then it all came gushing out. "Principal Martinez, it turns out I'm magical. I made Damien trip just by THINKING about it. I made it rain. I made cupcakes appear. I was having the best time ever.

But then my friend Olive was having a terrible time. So I went to the library. This book I found said that magic sometimes happens more to some people than others. So I got an idea that I could help Olive by giving her some of my magic. Only I didn't want to give her ALL of it. Just some of it. So we switched necklaces. Now everything has gone wrong. EVERYTHING. I don't know what to do."

Principal Martinez blinked at me for a while. I just waited.

"Let me get this straight," she said. "You flipped one of your classmates out of a beanbag chair because you lost your magic."

"Well, I mean . . . yes. See, normally Janice would never have sat there. If I still had my magic." That sounded a little silly when I said it out loud.

"And because you don't have your magic, you ripped off the tetherball." She looked at me over her glasses.

I cleared my throat. This was the look of truth. She did this a lot when I was in trouble.

I said a little quieter, "Uh . . . because it hit me in the head?"

I didn't like the way my voice went up at the end, like I wasn't sure. Principal Martinez was missing the point! She wasn't really listening to me. So I talked a little slower.

"Principal Martinez. Can. You. Help. Me. Or. Not?" I asked, staring hard at her.

Later, as I walked home from school, I thought about my three days of detention. And the fact that Principal Martinez hadn't answered my question.

SMILE!

hello

Chapter 8

Doing the Right Thing

Olive

Molly hadn't written to me for two days. That was weird. Sometimes we both got busy, but we always found time to send an email.

Something wasn't right.

I walked along our cow pasture. My favorite cow, Malick, came over and stuck her velvety nose over the wooden fence. I petted it. Her huge tongue gave me a big slobbery lick all up my arm.

I thought about all the good things that had happened to me over the past few days.

All of a sudden, Malick let out a big *MOO!* A scary moo! Malick was looking up, so I looked up too.

A tree branch was falling . . . fast.

I jumped out of the way. Malick moved. The branch fell right where I was standing! It could have hit me on the head and knocked me out.

I felt my necklace — Molly's necklace — and breathed deeply. It had to be the magic! Who knows what would have happened if I'd had on my other necklace.

Malick let out another moo. This time it was long and low. I jumped the fence and put my arms around her. Malick had saved me. Malick and the magic, of course.

The magic I had taken from Molly.

Tears pooled in my eyes. I had stolen magic from my best friend! That's probably why she wasn't talking to me. Bad things must be happening to *her* now. I had to give the necklace back.

But boy, I sure didn't want to.

I thought about the gymnastics meet — the bad one . . . Great-Aunt Gladys taking over my room . . . the rash . . . the neighbor's dog . . .

Then I thought about all those things happening to Molly. And I felt worse. I knew what I had to do.

I hugged Malick one more time, then ran to the house. I wrote a letter to Molly.

Dear Molly,

You have to take your necklace back. This is YOUR magic, and I can't take it. I'll figure out things on my own. You're the best friend ever for giving it to me. But I care about you too much to let you have bad luck.

Love,

Olive

Tears ran down my cheeks as I put the necklace in an envelope. But it was the right thing to do.

SEND MORE MAIL

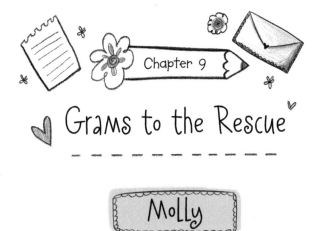

Chapter 9

Grams to the Rescue

Molly

My mom was NOT happy.

I knew this because I was doing the dishes after dinner. Then vacuuming the living room. Then cleaning DAMIEN'S ROOM, which was the worst thing of all.

She wouldn't even listen to me when I tried to explain. She heard the word "detention," and that was it. Now she was talking on the phone with Principal Martinez.

After a few minutes, things were quiet.

"Molly, come in here, please," Mom called.

I walked into the living room, dragging my feet. I sat on the chair across from her and crossed my arms. I couldn't look her in the eye. I'd had such rotten days lately. Now it was about to get worse.

"Dr. Martinez says you think you're in trouble because of magic," she said.

I shrugged.

"Molly," Mom went on, "did magic make you pick up that beanbag chair?"

"Well, in a way," I said.

Mom narrowed her eyes. "Did some outside force pick up your arms, march you over to that beanbag chair, and dump that poor girl out of it?"

"I . . . not exactly," I said. "But the magic made it so Janice sat there in the first place!"

"I don't care if a wizard appeared and put Janice into that beanbag chair. Molly Riley Graydon, did you or did you not flip your classmate out of a beanbag chair?"

I nodded.

"Then, first off, you're going to apologize to her. Second, you're going to use your own money to pay for a new tetherball rope."

Just then the apartment door opened. Grams walked in. I heard Damien run and fling himself at her.

Mom handed me a package. "And this came for you today. From Olive.

"We're done for now, but Molly, there's no such thing as magic. Not in the real world. I don't ever want to hear you using magic as an excuse for doing something again. You are responsible for yourself. Do you hear me?"

I nodded.

Mom hugged me, and I nestled my face in her neck a little. She whispered, "I love you, baby girl. Always." Then she kissed me on the head and went out to talk to Grams.

I ripped open the package from Olive. At least all of this would be worth it if things were going right for her. But when I opened the package, I couldn't believe my eyes.

She'd sent the necklace back. She'd figured out that my magic was gone.

That was SO Olive. She didn't want me to feel bad and get hurt.

I heard the door close, and Grams came in the room. She saw the look on my face and asked, "What's wrong, pumpkin?"

I told her everything.

When I told Grams about the magic, she said the OPPOSITE of what Mom had said. Kind of. She said, "Well, if you believe in something, sometimes it does come true. That's a type of magic. I bet we can find a way to fix this." Then she did an Internet search and got a candle and a bowl of salt water.

Grams had Damien and me sit with her in a circle. She put the bowl of salt water in the middle and lit the candle.

"Okay," she said, "the Internet says that we can 'cleanse' the necklaces. So, Molly, go ahead and drop them in."

I did.

Grams continued, "Now say, 'May the necklaces be cleansed!'"

I did. I yelled it, actually.

Grams winked at me and nodded at Damien to blow out the candle. "I think that's it," she said with a big smile.

The apartment was dark, except for the city lights twinkling through the windows. It really did feel magical.

Chapter 10

Back to Normal

Olive

Dear Olive,

Here is your necklace back. That was so nice to send me mine back. You're such a good friend. But guess what? I fixed your necklace!

My mom didn't believe in the magic at all. The book I found didn't have anything to help either. But my grandma knew what to do. It was really cool. She found a "cleansing" thing to do on the Internet. We cleaned out the bad energy, and the necklaces

should be safe now. According to the Internet and Grams anyway.

Best friends forever!

Love,

Molly

What a great surprise! This had to work. From what Molly had said before, her grandma was super smart about everything.

I put on my necklace, and I swear — I felt amazing right away!

All day at school, I kept track of things. When I got home, I wrote down what had happened and sent an email to Molly.

Molly!

Your plan was AWESOME! My day was full of good AND bad things. Here's what happened today:

Tyler stole my pencil.

Lila grabbed it from him and gave it back.

I got an A on a spelling test.

I got a B on a history test.

Lunch today was fabulous!

I spilled chili on my new sweater.

The bus was late coming to pick me up.

I got to write to you right after school (that's worth TWO good things).

So I think it's safe to say that our magic is perfectly balanced again. Unless you had a different day?

Love,

Olive

I got a response from Molly right away.

Dear Olive,

I think the magic is back to normal. I'll write more later. Right now I have to do a bunch of chores.

Love,

Molly

I shut down my computer and breathed deeply. The magic was back to normal.

The Coolest Magic There Is

Mom knocked and walked into my room.

"Honey, I'm really proud of you for taking responsibility," she said. "Do you see now that magic isn't real? It's really about making your own luck."

"But Mom, things were really magical for a while," I said. "There's no other explanation."

She put her arm around me. "Sure there is. That's just life. Sometimes good things happen, and sometimes bad things happen. It's what we do when those things happen — there's the REAL magic. We want to make sure we act wisely when good things and bad things happen. Do you know what I mean?"

I leaned into her. "Like, maybe ask Janice to move instead of dumping her out?"

Mom squeezed me. "Yes. Or, finding a different chair. What you and Olive have is very special. Both of you were willing to give up something for each other. I think that's the coolest magic there is." She winked at me and walked out the room.

She was right — what Olive and I had was the coolest thing ever. But that wasn't MAGIC. That was just being a good friend.

I moved to my computer, when out of the blue, a book fell from my book case, way across the room.

I walked over to it and looked down. It was the magic book! It had fallen open.

When I read the words on the page, I smiled and couldn't wait to tell Grams. Guess what chapter the book fell open to!

MAGIC IS REAL.

About the Author

Megan Atwood lives and works in Minneapolis, Minnesota. She has written more than 35 children's books and teaches creative writing at Hamline University. When she is not writing books or teaching, she is inflicting love and affection on her cats and dreaming up more characters to keep her company. She also is trying to find more time to write personal letters to her loved ones, much like Molly and Olive.

Megan Atwood

About the Illustrator

Lucy Fleming lives and works in a small town in England with an animator and a black cat. She has been an avid doodler and bookworm since early childhood, drawing every day, bringing characters and stories to life. She never dreamed that illustrating would be her job! When not at her desk, Lucy loves to be outdoors in the sunshine with a cup of hot tea — doodling, of course.

Lucy Fleming

Glossary

accidentally—without meaning to

apologize—to say "I'm sorry" for saying or doing something

back handspring—a kind of back flip

competition—a contest between two more people or teams

deserve—to earn something because of the way you act

detention—having to stay after school as punishment for doing something wrong

dismount—a move done to get off a piece of gymnastics equipment, such as a balance beam

pasture—land where farm animals eat and exercise

poison ivy—a plant that causes an itchy rash when touched

responsible—in charge

ruined—wrecked beyond repair

Talk It Out

1. Give at least three reasons why Molly thought she had magical powers.

2. If magic didn't help Olive score higher than Layna, what do you think did?

3. Explain the steps Grams, Molly, and Damien took to make the necklaces equal and good again.

Write It Out

1. Write your own short guide on how to use magic. Include helpful tips, rules, and warnings for your readers.

2. Make a list of all the good things that happened to you today. How were you responsible for those things happening?

3. If you had magical powers for one day only, how would you use them?

A Letter for You!

Dear friend,

My mom had a MAGICAL idea the other day (even if she doesn't think magic is real). See, she bakes amazing sugar cookies. THIS time she cut the cookies in star shapes and stuck cake-pop sticks in them. When they came out of the oven: ta-daa! Star wands! Damien and I got to decorate ours any way we wanted. So I used tons of pretty colored sugars and tied ribbons around the stick. Damien used just black sugar. He got it EVERYWHERE. It's probably good I don't REALLY have magic. Otherwise, I might have turned Damien into a toad by now.

Anyway, thanks for reading!

Yours truly,

Molly

The fun doesn't stop here!

Discover more at www.capstonekids.com

Videos & Contests

Games & Puzzles

Friends & Favorites

Authors & Illustrators

Find cool websites and more books like this one at www.facthound.com. Just type in the Book ID: 9781479586943 and you're ready to go!